MAXWELL MEMORIAL LIBRARY
14 GENESEE STREET
CAMILLUS, NY 13031

Table of Contents

Let's Play!	3
Photo Glossary	15
Index	16
About the Author	16

CAMILLUS

rourkeeducationalmedia.com

Can you find these words?

ball

cleats

goalie

team

Let's Play!

I play soccer.

I wear shin guards.

I run.

A **goalie** protects the net.

We score a goal!

team

My **team** gets one point.

Sometimes we win.
Sometimes we lose.

We always have fun!

Did you find these words?

I kick the **ball**.

I wear **cleats**.

A **goalie** protects the net.

My **team** gets one point.

Photo Glossary

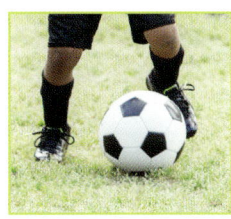 **ball** (bawl): A round object that is hit, thrown, or kicked in games.

 **cleats** (kleets): Special shoes for sports that have soles designed to keep the player from slipping.

 **goalie** (GOH-lee): Someone who guards the goal in soccer to keep the other team from scoring.

 **team** (teem): A group of people who work or play a sport together against another group.

Index

goal 10
kick 7
net 8

point 11
run 6
win 12

About the Author

Elliot Riley is the author of dozens of books for kids. When she's not reading or writing, you can find her walking by the water in sunny Tampa, Florida.

© 2019 Rourke Educational Media

All rights reserved. No part of this book may be reproduced or utilized in any form or by any means, electronic or mechanical including photocopying, recording, or by any information storage and retrieval system without permission in writing from the publisher.

www.rourkeeducationalmedia.com

PHOTO CREDITS: Cover: ©Gelner Tivadar; p2,7,12,14,15: ©kali9; p2,4,14,15: ©Yobro10; p2,8,14,15: ©mikkelwilliam; p2,11,14,15: ©Yuri_Arcurs; p3: ©FatCamera; p10: ©Baks

Edited by: Keli Sipperley
Cover and interior design by: Rhea Magaro-Wallace

Library of Congress PCN Data
Soccer / Elliot Riley
(Ready for Sports)
ISBN 978-1-64369-055-1 (hard cover)(alk. paper)
ISBN 978-1-64369-083-4 (soft cover)
ISBN 978-1-64369-202-9 (e-Book)
Library of Congress Control Number: 2018955860

Printed in the United States of America, North Mankato, Minnesota